MELLING, David

Stone goblins

ABOUT THE AUTHOR

David Melling was born in Oxford.
His first book was shortlisted for the Smarties
Book Award and The Kiss that Missed was
shortlisted for the Kate Greenaway Award.
He is married and lives with his wife
and children in Oxfordshire.

For more information, go to:
www.davidmelling.co.uk

Look
out for
all the
GOBLINS
books:

stone GOBLINS

David Melling

Hodder
Children's
Books

A division of Hachette Children's Books

First published in Great Britain in 2007
by Hodder Children's Books

All ch   nce

A Catalogue record for this book is available from the British Library

ISBN-13: 978 0 340 94408 0

Printed and bound in Germany by GGP Media GmbH

Hodder Children's Books
A division of Hachette Children's Books
338 Euston Road, London NW1 3BH
An Hachette Livre UK Company

Fingerprints by Monika and Luka Melling

For Claire Cartey

up

over there

over here

Down

Yak-Eating Dragon (run away)

Wandering Wood

plank

scale: 2 peeled bananas

There is a land, hidden but not so very far away, where the winds can blow day into night and most things inside out.

Nearly all the creatures in this secret place of magic and enchantment are friendly enough, in their own way, except, perhaps, for goblins.

Now, it is unwise to trust goblins of any kind, for they will lie and cheat as soon as look at you! But fortunately they are also dim-witted – as this story clearly shows ...

Introducing the Stone Goblins

Chief Cheesyfeet

Feet tightly bound to ensure that moist damp conditions are perfect for very cheesy smells. Always grumpy. Loves his mum.

Dribbledraws

Older brother of **Saggypant** and **Seepage** and father of **Damppatch** (left) and **Stain**.

Saggypant and Seepage
Twin brothers, tunnel guards and
a couple of prize plonks.

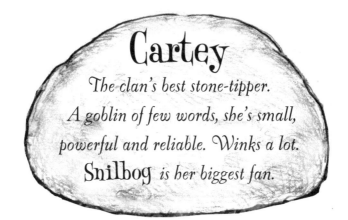

Cartey

The clan's best stone-tipper.
A goblin of few words, she's small,
powerful and reliable. Winks a lot.
Snilbog *is her biggest fan.*

Snilbog

Most goblins are nitwits, but **Snilbog** *can have the occasional good idea.* **Chief Cheesyfeet** *has recognised this and will often ask his advice. That way, he has someone to blame if it all goes wrong (which it usually does).*

When **Snilbog** is thinking he believes others see him like this ("The Thinker"):

... but really, he just looks as if he needs the loo. Loves to salute **Chief Cheesyfeet** and **Cartey**.

A FEW FACTS ABOUT STONE GOBLINS

⬭ HABITAT

Dark, smelly caves or tunnels, depending on size
of clan. Anywhere big enough to store as many
stones as possible.

⬭ CHARACTERISTICS

Love **stones**, an essential part of everyday life.

⬭ SLEEPING HABITS

Always sleep with their stone – it's better than
a best friend!

STONE-CARRYING TECHNIQUES

THE TUMMY HUGGER

THE BACK BREAKER

THE PLONKER

THE ART OF HUNTING, COOKING AND EATING

Like all goblins, Stone Goblins will eat just about anything – as long as it is small enough to be "splodged" by a stone.

Tea-time Tip: The Mushroom

(in 4 easy steps)

① **S**talk the unsuspecting mushroom by use of cunning camouflage. Pretend not to see the mushroom. A happy mushroom is easier to catch.

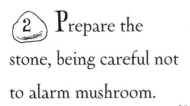

(2) Prepare the stone, being careful not to alarm mushroom.

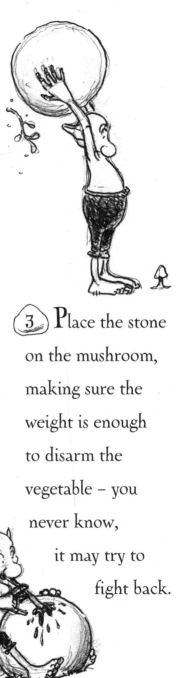

(3) Place the stone on the mushroom, making sure the weight is enough to disarm the vegetable – you never know, it may try to fight back.

(4) Turn stone over, thus creating a table. Make yourself comfortable, breathe hot fetid breath on mushroom for one minute (the cooking bit) and suck up with a straw.

◌ PRESSING

This goblin was caught making daisy chains, foolish thing. To teach him better manners, a heavy stone is "pressed" down on him. Three goblins will stand on top of the stone for at least five minutes. The stone is then lifted and planted.

The goblin will remain stuck to the stone for all to see – as a reminder of his silly behaviour. He will eventually slide to the floor. This usually takes no more than a day. Whilst he's waiting to peel away it gives us a chance to take a closer look at the typical Stone Goblin.

Tummy hair – curious fashion statement, tied with ribbon or plaits, and worn by some goblins, usually those in authority (presumably so they're important enough to hit anyone that laughs)

Large hands, feet and claws for digging (tunnels and noses)

Large head (plenty of room for small brain)

Big nose (for big fingers)

Large powerful arms – all goblins are VERY strong

Shoes and slippers – love to wear shoes and slippers, wherever they are found (they pinch each other's). Not unusual only to be wearing one, or to have a mixed pair

Contents

The Story Begins ...

There was once a gaggle of mountains, tall and proud, each with a hat of snow. And deep in their valleys sat a thick lake, like a bowl of lumpy porridge.

Beneath this lake lived a clan of Stone Goblins. Their hot and stuffy tunnels dripped like cracked pipes, and all the sights and sounds within were sucked up by a darkness so black that even the bats had to carry torches.

Stone Goblins only come above ground at night, unless someone goes missing. Then the stone-tippers are called upon to go topside. But even they can have problems …

Moonlight Surprise

An owl swooped down from her favourite tree on to a large stone. Funny, she thought, hadn't noticed this before. She looked at it more closely and noticed the feet. *Two* sets of feet, poking out either side of the stone. *Goblin* feet. She ruffled her feathers. She didn't like goblins. Best avoided.

One of the feet twitched, and a weak voice said, "Hello? Anybody there?" But there was no reply. The owl had already gone.

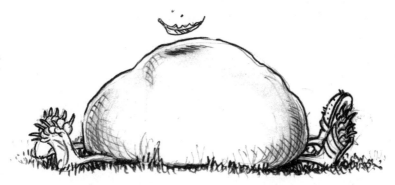

Chapter Two

Spider-Legs and Toenail Jam

Dribbledraws was not happy. He sat staring at his two little goblins, Damppatch and Stain, wrestling under the breakfast table. Normally he would be delighted with such behaviour, but today he was just not in the mood.

"Now come on you two, sit your bottoms down and eat your plucked spider-legs before they get cold."

"But it's not fair, he squished my earwig," whined Stain.

"Only because she squished mine," said Damppatch.

"Didn't, I just sat on it – a bit."

"I don't care who did what," growled Dribbledraws. "It's late and I has to take you to work today. Your mother's busy all day, tunnelling."

The little goblins stopped immediately and their two heads popped up, chins resting on the edge of the table.

4

"You mean we can go **topside** with you?"
they asked together.

"Well, I'm not sure you're ready to go *above*
ground, but maybe – if you're good."

Damppatch and Stain clambered on to their
stools, keen to show how good they could be.
They looked down at their
bowls of spider-legs.

"Why can't we
have something
else?" said
Damppatch.

5

"My friend Waft has toe-jam crackers, can't we have that?"

"Not today, my little whiff-breath, there isn't time. Oooh, *look*!" said Dribbledraws, trying to sound excited, "that leg is still *moving*! Now *please* eat – and remember, it's a race, so the first one to burp is the winner."

"But *look*!" said Damppatch. He plonked his foot on the table, making the bowls jump. "I've got loads of toe-jam under my toenails, you could make a whole sandwich with all that." Dribbledraws could smell the fetid feet; they really did honk. He was impressed.

"Oh, all right, I'll go get a fork and see what I can dig out – but then we leave, OK? And don't forget your table manners – I want to *see* and *hear* everything you're chewing."

Just then a low rumble sent the tables and chairs shivering across the room. It grew louder, then stopped abruptly.

"When I said I wanted to hear *everything*," growled Dribbledraws, "I didn't mean your toilet noises. We'll practise those later."

7

"It wasn't me!" said Damppatch and Stain together. Dribbledraws narrowed his eyes. They looked back at him with surprise – and, for once, he believed them.

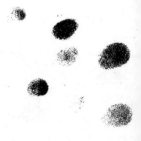

The Stone Room

Dribbledraws and his youngsters hurried
through the tunnels, the ground slowly
rising as they made their way topside.

To the little goblins, everything was new.
They cooed with excitement as they felt the air
change.

It was cooler and they noticed it had a
funny pong (they hadn't smelt fresh air
before).

At last, they saw their first squint of light
groping along the wet walls to meet them.

The tunnels echoed with their questions.

"What we going to do when we go topside?"

"*If* we go topside," said Dribbledraws,
"we'll collect a stone from the Stone Room and
practise hunting."

"Yeah!" the youngsters cheered.

"But we don't use the stone just to hunt, do
we?" said Damppatch. It was time to start
teaching them the ways of the Stone Goblin.
"We can also use it to hide from trouble."

"What kind of trouble?" asked Stain.

"Any kind of trouble!"
said Damppatch,

chopping the air with his hands.

"Of course, we may have to help a stone-tipper," said Dribbledraws.

"But what's a stone-tipper?" asked Stain.

"You don't know *nothing*," sneered Damppatch.

"More than you," said Stain, sticking out her tongue.

"A stone-tipper is someone who helps
a goblin if they gets stuck under their stone,"
said Damppatch. "If any goblins are missing
after a night of hunting, a stone-tipper will go
out and look for them, and help them if they
need it."

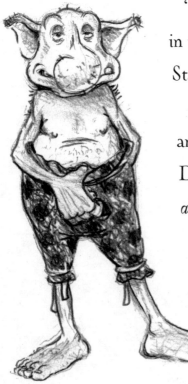

"But how do you get stuck
in the first place?" asked
Stain with a frown.

"Ask Uncle Saggypant
and Uncle Seepage," said
Damppatch. "They're
always getting stuck."

"Now, here we are at
the Stone Room,"
said Dribbledraws.
They went

through a small door and cooed again at how many stones lay there, piled high from floor to ceiling and from wall to wall.

Suddenly, the goblins noticed someone moving in the darker shadows of the room.

With a grin, the figure stepped into the thinner light by the door.

"Hello, Dribs, I've been looking for you."

"Hello, Snilbog. What's cooking?"

"Your brothers by the sound of it – got trapped again, and the stone was *enormous.*" Snilbog made a large circle with his arms.

"Told you, told you!" laughed Damppatch.

"What happened?"

"Looks like they chose a real whopper this time – no way they could carry it, but I guess they tried anyway."

Dribbledraws sighed. "They'll need rescuing, right?"

"That's exactly what they needs, Dribs, and no mistake," said Snilbog. "They'll be needing the stone-tippers for sure."

"Come on then, you two, let's go and see if we can help your uncles."

Snilbog nodded.

"Best hurry, Dribs me old mate, because Chief Cheesyfeet has heard about it. It's the third time this week, and old Cheesy is *really* cheesed-off."

"Can you hear something?" mumbled
Saggypant.

"Depends on what you had in mind – what
with being stuck under this great big stinking
boulder, and all," said Seepage.

"I think someone's coming, is
what I mean."

"About time – I
don't like it
under here.
I think I got a
worm what's
wriggled up
my nose."

"Oh, shut up and start
waggling your feet."

Chapter Four

Topside

Dribbledraws and his excited youngsters, both clutching little stones, finally emerged from the tunnel. They pinched their noses against the unfamiliar odours that swirled in the night breeze, surprised at how loud the sounds were that greeted them. They had grown up with a mixture of muffled tunnel noises and distant vibrations. Here, the topside world was alive with grasses that swished, branches that creaked and snail shells that cracked and squelched underfoot.

The little goblins had no idea fresh food could be so noisy.

They made their way to a small group of
goblins who stood muttering, hands on hips,
around a huge stone. Stain noticed a toe peeking
out from under the stone. It didn't look real. She
bent down and touched it quickly, and it wiggled
feebly back at her.

"Beats me how they managed to get it this
far," one goblin was saying. "They must have
been trying to bring it to the Stone Room."

"Only, the plonks didn't realise it was going to be too big to go down the hole!" laughed another.

"Doubt it will affect their brain box – methinks they haven't got many brains to squish."

"Oh, hello Dribbledraws," said one of the goblins, nudging his companion in the ribs. "Come to collect your brothers again? Got themselves in a right pickle this time and no mistake."

"Aye, looks that way, don't it?"

"We was just saying how we might get them out."

"Well," said Dribbledraws. He puffed out his cheeks. "I've never seen a stone this big." He was quiet for a minute, hands on hips.

Then, slowly shaking his head, he sighed.
"There's only one thing we can do." There was
a hush among the stone-tippers. They knew what
was coming. "We better get Cartey!"

There was a general muttering of agreement.

Dribbledraws cupped his hands to his mouth
and cried,

"Get Cartey!"

This was shouted back along the line of
goblins, gradually disappearing down the
tunnel as a series of echoes. They grew fainter,
only to grow louder again, this time with the
reply:

"she's on her way!"

"Who's Cartey?" asked Stain nervously.

"Only the best stone-tipper we have,"
beamed Snilbog, who had just arrived.

"If anyone can rescue the twins, she can!" He stood to attention with a click of his heels, raised his hand in salute and waited. He liked Cartey.

Moments passed as the goblins waited. Then a low rumble started. The ground shivered and loose rubble danced around the entrance to the tunnel.

"There's nothing to worry about," said Dribbledraws. Damppatch and Stain leaned against him, unsure.

"She's as soft as mud really. We call her Cartey because she carries her tipping tools in a cart wherever she goes. There's no messing with her, mind you, so don't get in her way!"

Finally Cartey appeared, blinking her yellow eyes in the daylight. She looked smaller than the little goblins had been expecting, but thick-set and strong. As she passed, Stain noticed she smelt of baked beans. They realised that the large clanky tools bouncing around inside the rickety cart had made her sound much bigger!

"Hello, Cartey," squeaked Snilbog with a stiff grin.

Cartey winked at him as she lumbered past.

Saggypant and Seepage

Damppatch and Stain watched Cartey in silence. She stood there patting, stroking and smelling the giant stone. Snilbog noticed she was mumbling something quietly to herself. She's so fab, he thought.

"My, my, my!" Cartey said, her eyes moving over the stone. "What kind of fools would try to carry this here lump of rock?" She crouched down and looked at the same toe that Stain had touched. She pulled it like an elastic band and let it go with a twang. This time the toe wiggled with more energy.

"I knows this toe – don't I, Saggypant?"

she roared, leaning against the stone. Giving the toe a pat, she said, "We'll have you two plonks out from under there in no time, hehe!"

Cartey rummaged around in her cart and pulled out a selection of tools. She wedged a "stick-thingy", as she called it, under the stone and, to the amazement of the gathering crowd, she twisted, turned and lifted it with no more

than a grunt. The stone rose up and rolled to the side with a dull thud.

It had left a large crater. The stone-tippers shuffled forward and peered in. No one spoke for a long time.

"Are they supposed to look like that?" one goblin asked.

Dribbledraws helped the groggy twins to their feet. Luckily the ground was soft, which had certainly saved their lives, and two perfect twin prints were left where they had lain.

It took the twins five minutes to stand up without any help, and then, shaking and dizzy, they gradually explained to everyone what had happened.

"We was thinking how good it would be to bring home this here stone," said Saggypant, "but *Sneezy* here," pointing to his brother, "had a nose dribble and the next thing I knows this great thing comes crashing down on me." He gave it a kick, then hopped around, howling with pain.

"Ooooh – you fibber!" spluttered Seepage. "There's me holding *my* end when *Twinkle-toes* here bends down to pick up a daisy, if you please."

There was a gasp from the other goblins.

"I never did and you take that back!" said Saggypant, his face turning pink. A white flower petal fluttered to the ground and he covered it quickly with his foot.

"That's enough of that, you nitwits!" said Snilbog. "Be careful what you say – here comes Chief Cheesyfeet."

Everybody bowed their head and dropped to one knee. Damppatch and Stain had never seen the Chief before and weren't prepared for what they saw.

Balancing on top of a pile of stones and carried by a pair of stone-bearers, Chief Cheesyfeet, a small goblin with an enormous nose, looked as if he would topple over at any moment. But he appeared quite comfortable, and glared down at the twins as he waited for an explanation.

Half an hour later, Saggypant and Seepage were acting out exactly how a wonky-beaked eagle (actually, it was a moth) had attacked them, just as they were about to catch a vicious bear (a mouse) for their tea.

Chief Cheesyfeet was tapping his foot irritably.

"Cor!" said a wide-eyed goblin, "and we thought you gone and picked up a stone what was too big-like."

"They *did*, you idiots," growled Chief Cheesyfeet. "Now let's all get back down the tunnel before a *real* wonky-beaked eagle comes flying past looking for a mid-morning snack."

Saggypant and Seepage leaned against the stone in relief, satisfied that they'd managed to avoid getting into too much trouble with their chief.

But Cartey was on her hands and knees inside the crater, carefully balancing the stone with her tipping tools, ready to start rolling it away.

Now, with a creak and a dull thud, the stone rolled back on to the spot where the twins had been trapped.

It was some moments before Dribbledraws said, "Er … anybody seen Cartey?"

Cartey's Brain

hief Cheesyfeet was so cross, his trousers fell down. This made him even madder and he hopped around shouting at everyone.

Somehow, a team of stone-tippers managed to lift the stone and grab Cartey by the ankles just before it came crashing down again. They plopped her on the cart and took her downside.

Now, Stone Goblins don't have doctors. The closest thing they have is a goblin medic known as Bop-a-Top. He believes he has the magic power to take away any goblin's pain.

His method is to hit (bop) the patient's head (top) with a mallet. Of course, he usually knocks the poor goblin unconscious, so by the time they wake up at least the original pain is gone and long forgotten (together with the memory, usually).

Bop-a-Top looked into Cartey's

eyes as they rolled lazily round in circles. They seemed to be moving in different directions. Since the stone had landed on her head, another bop was probably not a good idea.

He decided to give it a try anyway – but Dribbledraws pulled his ears just as Bop-a-Top was swinging the mallet. Bop-a-Top lost his balance and fell backwards, flipping the mallet high into the air. He landed on his back and watched it come tumbling down towards him.

"No!" he managed to say very quietly, just before it landed on his nut. He didn't wake up for a week.

Chief Cheesyfeet was pacing his throne-room. He had seen Bop-a-Top dragged past his door moments earlier.

Now Saggypant, Seepage and Snilbog stood before him: Two plonks and a plank, he thought. He took a closer look at the twins and wondered if the effects of being trapped under a stone the size of a buffalo for ten hours had worn off. He honestly couldn't tell.

"Well?" he said at last.

Snilbog was still too upset at the state of Cartey's brain to speak, so Seepage coughed and stepped forward. "Truth is, boss," he said carefully, "old Cartey's been well and truly hammered, and she is a little scrambled up top." He tapped his head with two fingers. "That is to say, we think her brain's got a bit … er, loose."

"Mashed banana for brains is what you said," interrupted Saggypant helpfully. Snilbog whimpered and bit his knuckles.

Seepage frowned and quickly added, "She is speaking well enough, only," he paused, "not all the words are in the right order."

Saggypant noticed the Chief wasn't sharing their smiles and added, "She can still clean her tooth – as long as someone else does the brushing."

Chief Cheesyfeet slumped back in his chair with a groan. "How long before she—"

But he didn't get to finish. There came a sudden burst of something like thunder, so loud it sounded as if it was inside the tunnel.

"Now what?" said the chief, brushing rubble from his shoulders.

It happened again. And again. The noises continued for what seemed like hours, before finally coming to an abrupt halt.

Chief Cheesyfeet got up. Snilbog was standing to attention in the middle of the room, covered in dust. He decided to get a grip – Cartey would be fine. The others were huddled together in the corner.

"It is my considered opinion," Snilbog began, "that we should investigate the noises as soon as we possibly can, boss, on account of them being unusual and possibly dangerous to our well-being—"

"Yes, yes, *yes*," snapped Chief Cheesyfeet. "Will you stop waffling on?"

He peered into the eyes of Snilbog, who seemed not to have moved during what appeared to be an earthquake. He wondered, not for the first time, why he encouraged the company and advice of such a first-class plonk.

Mind you, he thought, when things go wrong (which seemed to be happening more and more lately), he always had somewhere to point the finger of blame. He sighed and looked around the room for the other fools.

"Now then," he said, brushing himself down and briefly disappearing in a cloud of dust, "I'll need two idiots – I mean, volunteers – to check out the tunnels and report back to me as soon as possible."

Earthquakes and Lost Teeth

Saggypant and Seepage had been groping around the tunnels for about ten minutes when they gave up and sat down to pick their toenails.

"I'm really bored," moaned Saggypant. "What we looking for anyway?"

"Whatever made them noises, is what Cheesyfeet told us. Some kind of trouble, whatever it is," said Seepage.

"What *kind* of trouble, Seeps?" asked Saggypant, squinting into the blackness. (He was actually facing the wall.)

"How do I know?"

"Aha!" guffed Saggypant. "Is it black and greasy – because if it is, I think I found it?"

"That's my hair, you idiot," growled Seepage.

"How do I know you're

not just *pretending* to be my brother," said
Saggypant, and tightened his grip.

"Let go my hair or I'll give you such a wallop,"
said Seepage, sticking his elbow out.

"Ooommphh! Why, you!" Saggypant yanked
his brother's hair.

"Aarrgh!" roared Seepage. He grabbed
something soft and bit it hard!

With squeals of rage the brothers rolled
around the floor in a tight ball, growling
and spitting.

Suddenly, the ground above them
trembled and growled again. The noises
seemed *very* close.

The brothers stopped fighting and
stood up quickly, like two naughty children
caught doing something wrong.

43

"What's that then?" said Saggypant.

"Don't know, but it isn't right," said Seepage, looking at the floor. He slowly lifted one foot at a time, to see if the noise would go away.

It didn't.

"Worms, maybe?" asked Saggypant hopefully.

The noise grew louder and seemed to surround them. Chunks of the ceiling started crumbling and bits of it bounced off their heads.

Saggypant held out a hand as if testing for rain. "If the ceiling comes down, do you think we'll get wet, on account of there being that great big lake topside?"

"I don't know about that, but I think we're going to find out what's making that noise any minute," said Seepage.

44

"I think you're right, Seeps!" Saggypant said.
He pulled out his lucky stick and jabbed it at
the dark.

Seepage joined him and linked arms.

"Who's out there?" they shouted, dancing a little jig they hoped looked threatening. "Come on, show yourself! We're ready for you!"

It was just about the last sensible thing they said, heard, or thought about for quite some time. In the next instant the vibrating tunnel came alive, rumbling and crumbling all around them. The twins felt like they were in the throat of a giant beast.

"I DoN'T tHiNk ThiS iS nOrMaL?" quivered Seepage.

The brothers wobbled violently. Their goblin teeth shook loose from their gums and fell from their mouths, lost to the darkness. (Which was fine, because you don't need teeth to scream.)

A split second later a large section of the ceiling, just above their heads, opened up with a very loud "**POP!**" They could just make out a watery circle of light before a tonne of lumpy lake came crashing down, flushing them along the tunnel like two peas in a hosepipe.

They were spat out of the tunnel where they joined the rest of the clan, dazed and confused.

A Yak-Eating Dragon's Tail

T he twins found themselves covered in the thick, foul-smelling mud that was once their topside lake. They clawed their way back to the tunnel opening but found it blocked by a muddy lump of something. They sat on it, exhausted with the effort, then sprang up wildly when the something moved.

It was Chief Cheesyfeet. His face – what they could see of it – was purple with rage.

"Has this got anything to do with you two?" he growled.

49

"No, Chief, honest!" they said together.

Chief Cheesyfeet managed to stand up. He peeled drying clumps of mud from his body and, turning to the tunnel opening, peered inside. The walls were clogged with thick, dripping, stringy globules of mud. It was like looking into a giant yawning mouth of half-chewed food. And the smell!

"Wow – not bad!" he said cheerfully. He felt better already. "Would have taken years to get it looking this good. Right, follow me everyone!"

The smell was like stale snail. It was stronger inside the hot tunnel and hung in the air with nowhere to go. Chief Cheesyfeet sniffed long and hard. "Reminds me of my old mum," he said, blinking tears.

Ankle-deep, he waded deeper along the

tunnel, a train of goblins behind him.

When he stopped sharp, several goblins bundled into him. He slapped them back and told them to zip it.

Up ahead, fat and limp, lay what looked like a dragon's tail.

"How did *that* get in here?" said Chief Cheesyfeet, scratching his head. "I mean, usually there's a dirty great big dragon at the other end of one of these!"

"Hmmm, interesting question, boss," said Snilbog. "Maybe it's a snake that swallowed a dragon's tail. You know, like they do with eggs – you can always see when a snake has eaten an egg, because they have this big round bit in their tum—" Snilbog stopped when he saw Chief Cheesyfeet's face.

"You need the loo, boss? Only, you got a funny look about you."

"Shut up, you plonk!" growled Cheesyfeet. "Now listen, I want this thing out of my tunnel by the end of the day, get it?"

"Yes, boss."

"Oh, and Snilbog?"

"Yes, boss?"

"Let me know if you find the other end, won't you?"

"Yes, boss!"

Inside the Dragon's Tummy

S nilbog sat down to think about what to do.
He liked to call himself "The Thinker" and
he knew the Chief relied on him to come up
with good ideas.

Everyone gathered round to see if they could
actually hear Snilbog's brain muscle moving.

"Stand back, all of you," said Chief
Cheesyfeet. "Give him space – brains need
air if they're gonna work proper. And you lot
sure got plenty of air inside your nuts," he
mumbled to himself.

It was quite a while before Snilbog finally
raised a thoughtful finger and said, "Y'know,

boss, how about me and some of the lads go topside. Maybe something's happened with the lake?"

Brilliant, thought Chief Cheesyfeet, even I could have come up with that one. But he nodded, then with a smile, turned and looked at Saggypant and Seepage. "Take these two idiots with you before they do any more damage downside."

The brothers stood to attention. They were trying not to speak. After they'd lost their teeth in the tunnel, they'd decided to try using some small stones from the Stone Room instead. Speech wasn't easy. It was like talking with a mouthful of marbles.

Five minutes later, Snilbog and the two brothers emerged into the evening air, crawled up the slight incline and looked into the bowl where the lake used to be.

Saggypant's parents had nearly given him the name Trump, and for good reason. He did one now, when he realised what he was looking at.

"Well knobble my knees – a **dragon**!" squeaked Snilbog, "an' it's a BIGGY!"

But it was too much for the twins. They had already legged it back downside. Stone Goblins find comfort in the dark.

Snilbog rolled his eyes. "Typical," he muttered. He climbed into the empty lake and, with bold but muddy steps, he made his way slowly towards the dragon.

Now, the dragon was a rare female yak-eating dragon. She had spotted the lake whilst out yak-hunting, and was keen to get rid of a big hairball that was stuck at the back of her throat. (If you mostly eat hairy yaks, you really do need a good gargle every now and then.) And she had decided to take a break and have a bit of a splash about at the same time.

Well, she was enjoying herself so much she started to hum a low rumbling tune (which, of course, was one of the noises that was upsetting the goblins so much). And she was so busy humming and splashing and gargling, she didn't notice when one of her long curly talons caught on something in the sludge at the bottom of the lake.

It was an ancient chain, forged by goblins at a time when the mountains were only lumps in the grass.

The dragon pulled it
free of the sludge
and there, dangling
from her talon, was
a plug! The next
moment the thick
water began to
swirl and gurgle
and bubble
around her.

Slowly, the
clotted lake
disappeared.

Dragons can be
very slow thinkers,
and she was still
trying to work out
what had happened an
hour later when the
tide-mark of mud around her
middle had almost dried. She
heard a cough and turned
round, irritable and confused.
A little goblin was looking up at her.

"Oi, Scaly!" it said. "Can we have our lake
back please?" (Truth be told, Snilbog was quite

good at solving problems, but not so good at judging someone's mood.)

The dragon bent down and swallowed him whole!

But goblins are smelly grubby creatures for good reason. When goblin-hair comes into contact with the saliva of any other animal, it stiffens as sharp as needles and oozes a sticky gloop that even a dragon's tummy cannot handle. The dragon belched Snilbog up and out, together with an eggy-burp of such horror, she shivered and keeled over in a dead faint.

Snilbog was covered in the dragon's tummy-juices, but very much alive. He sat up and pulled a half-digested carrot from his ear (even yak-eating dragons know that vegetables are good for you). Then he got to his feet and made his way, with slow sticky-saliva steps, back underground for a chat with the Chief.

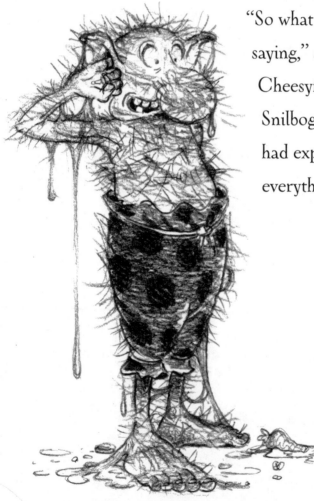

"So what you're saying," said Chief Cheesyfeet, when Snilbog had explained everything, "is that we got a dragon's tail down here with us, and a big fat dragon topside … in a lake … what's got no water?"

Snilbog appeared to be glazed from head to foot in chewed yak hair, but Chief Cheesyfeet decided not to say anything.

"That is exactly the situation how I sees it, boss – and no mistake."

"Then, my question to you … is this," said Chief Cheesyfeet carefully. "Is there any way of finding out if the tail *here* and the dragon up *there* are in any way connected?"

Snilbog frowned. Eventually, his eyes widened and he clicked his fingers. "Ooooh, you mean all joined-up like? Yeah, you got something there, boss! You know, I bet they are!"

"Right then," said Chief Cheesyfeet in a loud voice. "In that case, I want two volunteers to go out there and tell that dragon to SHOVE OFF! Any offers?"

Chapter Ten

Inside the Dragon's Tummy – Again!

Two minutes later, Saggypant and Seepage pushed each other out of the tunnel.

"*I* didn't volunteer," said Saggypant. "I was just shushing a fly off me."

"Then why didn't you say so, you turnip?" said Seepage.

"Because you said don't speak to no one until we can speak proper with our new teeth, or everyone will laugh at us."

"Well, we *can th*speak proper now, can't we?" spluttered Seepage.

The brothers continued to argue all the way to the side of the lake … until Saggypant

pointed out a pair of green eyes watching
them. They both yelped and jumped behind
a rock.

The dragon glared at the rock, which seemed
to sprout two goblin-shaped ears as Saggypant
and Seepage peered over the top.

"It's *humming*!" hissed Seepage. "Can you
believe it?" He gave Saggypant a prod. "Go on
then, it's looking at you – you go!"

"Do WHAT?" squawked Saggypant. "But it
isn't my turn!"

But before he could argue any
more, Seepage pushed him from
behind the stone.

He found himself looking up into
the hungry eyes of the yak-eating dragon.

So he did the only thing he could do – he fainted.

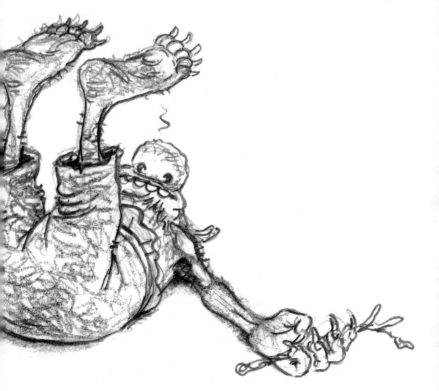

The dragon leaned forward, curious. But Seepage sprang out from behind the rock and charged. "You leave my brother alone!"

Delighted to have another chance to eat a goblin, the dragon got down on all fours, opened her mouth and rolled out her tongue.

Seepage had lowered his head and was too busy
keeping his eyes as tightly shut as possible to
notice where he was going.

He ran straight on to the dragon's tongue,
into her mouth, down her throat and landed
with a splash in a warm and bubbly digesting
broth. Within moments, the mingling of stiff
goblin-hair and dragon tummy-juices
propelled Seepage back up and out
of the dragon's mouth. Another
belch of eggy-breath lifted
him high into the air. And,
for a second time, the
dragon fainted.

When Seepage landed, he noticed he was clutching a yak's tooth. That's handy, he thought. Why bother with lots of teeth when you can have one big one?

He picked off some of the pink wobbly bits, gave it a quick wipe and popped it in his mouth. He pushed it around with his tongue, trying to find a comfortable spot. Then he licked his lips and had a go at speaking.

"Thammph!" he drooled. Perfect! he thought. With a bit of practice no one will be any the wiser. And at least I can smile again.

He made his way back to Saggypant, who was sitting on

top of the snoring dragon and pounding his fists on her tummy.

"Hang on, Seeps – I'm coming to get you!" he sobbed. He stood up and tried to head-butt his way through the dragon's scaly tummy.

Seepage was touched by the gesture.

"Oi – thwapat goolie pif!" he dribbled.

Saggypant, tears running down his cheeks, looked up and saw his brother. With a yelp of delight he slid off the dragon and they both hugged.

When Saggypant let go, he noticed something odd about his brother's face.

He seemed to be grinning in a very unusual way.

Saggypant's eye followed a trail of dragon spittle as it dribbled down his brother's cheek. Then he noticed the yak's tooth.

"Where did you get that from?" he demanded.

"In*th*ide the dragon'*th* tummy – it'*th* a yak'*th* tooth," Seepage said proudly.

"I can see that," said Saggypant. "Some goblins have all the luck!"

Never Wake a Sleeping Dragon

T he twins knew that if they returned to the tunnels without getting rid of the dragon, Chief Cheesyfeet might send them topside for good. The thought of hiding in daylight from the dragon that had already tried eating them twice was not a happy one. They might not be so lucky next time. The beast was still lying on her back in a dead faint, but they needed to think of something quickly. Then they might solve the problem *and* be heroes.

"Ooooh, is it dead?" came a voice from behind them. The twins twirled around and saw Damppatch and Stain creeping towards them.

They were trying to hide behind a branch
of leaves.

"Cor, it's *so* big!"

"What are *you* two doing here?" said
Seepage. The brothers grabbed one goblin each
and bundled them behind a rock.

"Dribbledraws said we couldn't go and see
the dragon – said it was too dangerous," said
Damppatch.

"It's not fair," said Stain, "so
we decided to come look for
ourselves."

"Er, I don't think that's such
a good idea," said Seepage.
"Your dad will go mad if he sees you
up here."

"Absolutely," agreed Saggypant.

"*I'll* take them back, Seeps, and you sort out the dragon, right?"

"How does *that* work?" squawked Seepage. "We'll *all* go back down the tunnels and pretend it's gone away. Then maybe when we come back later it won't be here no more."

He had already given up the idea of being a hero.

The four goblins crept slowly around the head of the sleeping dragon. Damppatch's attention was caught by the different-coloured scales of the dragon's eyelids – when, to his horror, they flicked open. All four goblins froze in a moment of pure terror.

Saggypant managed to find his voice, just as the dragon rose.

"RUN!" he cried.

The four goblins scattered.

Now, the goblins thought that the dragon would be furious and ready to eat them with a flick of her tongue. But the truth was, she had had just about enough of goblins. They had a nasty habit of jumping out of her tummy when she thought they were good and eaten, and where that evil eggy taste had come from she *really* didn't want to think about. So now, looking down at four of the horrible creatures running around in circles, well, it gave her the willies.

She was suddenly aware that she couldn't stand properly. Somehow, her tail was stuck in some kind of muddy hole. She looked around with growing panic. Now she could only see one goblin. Where had the other three got too? She roared and tried to stand again.

Down on the ground, Saggypant was in the same blind panic. He had lost sight of the others and the dragon had let rip with the most terrifying roar.

"This is it," he groaned. "I'm going to be eaten, chewed and spat out just like … Seepage was last time!"

As soon as he said it, he realised it was true – Seepage *had* been spat out. He also remembered the same happening to Snilbog. Maybe she doesn't like the taste of goblin, he thought.

"As long as I can avoid the *chewing* part of being eaten, I *should* be OK," he mumbled to himself. He pulled out his lucky stick and waved it about at the dragon. But he had closed his eyes and couldn't see where he was going. He stumbled forward and bumped clumsily into the belly of the dragon.

Now it's a well-known fact (except to goblins) that all dragons have one "scale soft-spot" on their body. But it is in a different place on each creature, making it very difficult to find if you happen to be fighting a dragon in your spare time. It could be anywhere. And it is the one squishy bit where they *really* don't like being touched (gives them terrible wind, apparently).

So it was pure luck that Saggypant found this scale and poked it when he tripped up. With a

howWWWWWWWWl

and a

roooaaaaaaRRRRRRRR

the dragon leapt into the air, freeing herself from the tunnel with an almighty **POP!**

She launched into the air and disappeared
over the mountain tops as fast as she could, the
chain and plug still
trailing behind her.

Chapter
Twelve

From Idiots to Heroes – and Back Again

Seepage joined his brother as they watched the
dragon go. They hugged and shouted and
danced with joy, until their legs got tangled and
they ended up fighting each other in an effort to
free themselves.

Damppatch and Stain, who had seen
everything, ran to the tunnels and called
Dribbledraws to come see what had happened.

The twins sat and waited. They couldn't decide
whether to be happy about getting rid of the
dragon, or cross about getting tangled up again.

Then the echoey voice of Chief Cheesyfeet
boomed up from the tunnel.

"If you two idiots are still alive, will you please tell me what's going on up there! And if that's you, Mr Dragon," his voice softer and sprinkled with rose-petals, "would you mind awfully if I ask you go away and leave our plughole alone - thanking you!"

When the Stone Goblins realised that the dragon had gone, they all came out to join the twins. Damppatch and Stain told everyone how Seepage had grabbed them from the terrible jaws of the dragon whilst Saggypant had poked it with his stick. The brothers couldn't quite remember it the same way, but with each telling they sounded braver and braver, so they decided to keep quiet.

"OF COURSE," said Snilbog in a loud

voice – it was unusual to have the whole clan together in one place and he wanted to show off his brain muscles – "all we need now is a new plug and a lot of rain."

"You mean, the dragon took the plug with it?" asked Dribbledraws.

"Exactly," said Snilbog.

"In that case," said Chief Cheesyfeet, "we need one or two of you to stick yourselves down the plughole and block it up, so as we can fill up the lake as soon as possible. Any volunteers?"

That night, as Saggypant and Seepage hung upside down in the plughole, they were so cross they refused to talk to each other.

This was just as well, because they were wedged together as tight as pants and could hardly breathe, let alone speak.

When Chief Cheesyfeet had asked for volunteers, it had made Seepage jump. Unfortunately, he'd swallowed his yak's tooth, which then made him cough so loudly that the Chief thought he was trying to get his attention. And when Chief Cheesyfeet asked them if they were volunteering *again*, Saggypant was so scared he pasted a frozen grin on his face. Chief Cheesyfeet thought he meant, "*Yes please!*"

It would take two months to forge a new plug, and during that time the rains would come and the lake would fill again. The twins were assigned a guard whose job it was to put food into their mouths as often as they liked – so it wasn't all bad.

Meanwhile, Cartey was making good progress. Dribbledraws was helping her get her memory back, and everyone had high hopes that one day she would be their best stone-tipper again.

She certainly showed a lot of interest in tipping. Unfortunately, she was still a little mixed-up and liked to tip stones *on* to goblins. Only time would tell if this would change.

Dribbledraws was cross with Damppatch and Stain for running away, but pleased that they had been involved in the famous Yak-Eating Dragon story. It would be told around campfires for years to come.

"I have a question," said Chief Cheesyfeet to Snilbog one morning, as they were eating mashed slug on toast for breakfast. "How we going to swap those two idiots for the plug, now that the lake is full of water again?"

There was a long, long silence … followed by more silence.

"Er …!" said Snilbog.

Epilogue

This story is very old. In fact, *so* old that Stone Goblins today laugh at the work of a stone-tipper. The modern Stone Goblin has trained woodlice and worms to do this job. These creatures tunnel their way under the stone and loosen enough earth for a goblin to rescue the trapped idiot from underground. This way, they can avoid going topside and being on the menu of the wonky-beaked eagle.

So if you turn over a stone and find a family of woodlice or the odd worm, you have probably just missed seeing a trapped Stone Goblin.

But keep looking – one day, you might be lucky!

Shilbog's Guide to Stone Tipping

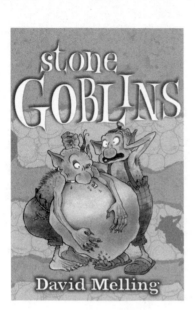

stone GOBLINS

David Melling

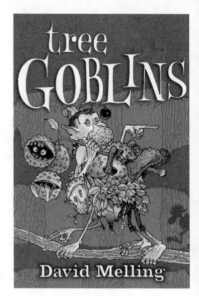

tree GOBLINS

David Melling

COLLECT

THEM ALL!

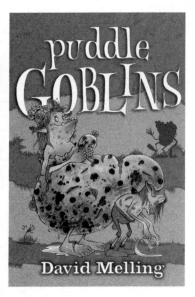

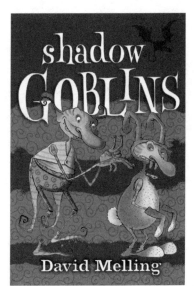

some
goblin
sketches

Piggy-Piggy BadBack.

Tunnell Goblins

(they don't get out much...)

Gloves for digging

A Plonk and a Plònk (take yer pick.)

OOPS!

"**Of all the silly, nitwitted, knobbly-nosed, gobbledegooked plonks I've ever come across, YOU, Mr Butterfingers, take the biscuit!**"

It was Mildew who'd just fallen out of the tree. She lay sprawled on the ground, still clutching her eggs.

Sitting up, she arranged the eggs carefully next to her, and began picking out bits of twig from some of the more uncomfortable places.

"What happened?" came a voice, groggy and muffled with leaves.

"I would have thought," said Mildew, "that was obvious."

Butterfingers went quiet and tried to think. Whenever they fell out of the tree, it always took him a few moments to rewind his memory and work out exactly how it had happened. He closed his eyes and this is what he saw:

Butterfingers, a little hungry, stands up to reach a beetle.

Mildew falls out.

Butterfingers tries to catch her on her way down.

He loses his balance and tumbles after her.

Mildew lands first, with a bounce.

Followed by Butterfingers.

Mildew lands on Butterfingers on the second bounce.

Butterfingers is now pressed firmly into the soft earth.

Mildew (finally) stops bouncing.